Ted was having a bath in the sink because he'd had an adventure in the mud.

"It's past one o'clock, Dad. When's lunch?" asked Sam. "When I can think of a plan," said Dad.

Nan dried her hands and had a
look. "Not much in here," she said.
"True," said Dad.
"The issue," said Nan, "is that
we are due – overdue – to go
shopping."

Sam lifted Ted from his bath and joined in. He got out three old carrots, a hard lump of blue cheese, a sliver of lemon, a dab of butter, a bit of milk, and the heel of a loaf.

They looked at them.
"Bingo!" said Dad. "I say,
'Hello, lunch!'"

"But the blue cheese ..." said Sam.
"I agree it's a bit firm."
"Firm? It's rock hard, Dad! You
can't cook it, it will be like glue."
"Just you wait. I have a clever plan
to whizz up a fondue feast."

"So, first, Sam," said Dad, "run the carrot under the water. Second, peel it. Third, chop it into chunks – fingers out of the way."

Dad stirred the butter in a pan and added milk and water. He cut in the cheese and squeezed the lemon.

He handed Sam the spoon. "Fondue means melted, so you fold and stir, fold and stir so that the blue cheese melts, not burns."

Nan cut up the heel of the loaf
and toasted it. She found her old
fondue forks.

"Let's eat!" said Dad. They pronged and dipped until all the fondue was eaten up.

"That will keep us going for the rest of the afternoon," said Dad. "Now for that overdue shopping list. What do we need?"